YOU
RUINED
IT

Other books by Anastasia Higginbotham

Death Is Stupid

Divorce Is the Worst

Not My Idea

Tell Me About Sex, Grandma

What You Don't Know

YOU RUINED IT

By Anastasia Higginbotham

dottir press
NEW YORK

Published in 2022 by Dottir Press
33 Fifth Avenue
New York, NY 10003

Dottirpress.com

First printing

Angeliska's spell on page 65 is from *Starhawk. The Spiral Dance: A Rebirth
of the Ancient Religion of the Great Goddess*. 10th anniversary ed., with
new introd. and chapter-by-chapter commentary. HarperSanFrancisco,
1989. p. 140.

Illustrations and text by Anastasia Higginbotham
Production by Drew Stevens and Frances Ross

Trade distribution through Consortium Book Sales and Distribution,
www.cbsd.com.

Library of Congress Cataloging-in-Publication Data is available for this title.

ISBN 978-1-948340-30-4
eBook available

PRINTED IN THE UNITED STATES OF AMERICA BY WORZALLA

for every child who never told,
who told but wasn't believed,
who paid a price for telling,
who paid a price for not knowing
there was something to tell
to begin with, and
for every child who,
in the words of
Lynda Barry
"can't remember,"
can't forget
this book is for you and me ♥

♥ Our bodies know.

Our bodies know the truth.

⋛ IDEAS ⋚
for how to settle as you engage
with this book, these characters,
and this story as it unfolds:

love
is my
lineage

(1.) The child in this
story practices
returning
attention and awareness
to their body,
breath, and belly
as a way to stay
~ connected and
whole ~
when they are
frightened or
stressed right
out of themselves.

This returning to
⟿ yourself, your body,
over and over again, is
something I practice ~ thanks
to Reverend angel Kyodo williams.

⋛ YOU CAN TOO. ⋚

"come back to yourself." - Rev.
angel ♥

2.

There are exercises you can do to soothe and hold yourself when you feel upset and as you heal from any trauma.

To learn and practice some of these exercises, go to @twinpowerment where Nell and Tish demonstrate and teach a lot of ways we can care for ourselves.

With both hands, make light fists.
Start at your lower waist or groin area and begin tapping in place.

Dear One,

This book does not depict the violence that has happened.

It is a story that addresses incest and betrayal in the gentlest way I could imagine doing.

It is one of the ordinary, terrible things that can sometimes happen in a child's life.

In this story, the person who commits the crime is only a little older than a child themselves, and it is likely someone committed the same crime against them when they were younger because that is sometimes how it goes.

And goes and goes...

In this story, **it stops.** The abuse is not excused or allowed to continue.

As you read or listen to and take in the images of the story, notice what is happening in your body.

Do you feel warm, cold, tingly, numb, sad, scared, mad? Anything tugging or churning, roiling or rising in you?

Do you want to close the book and put it away for now? You can.

You are the one who decides whether to keep going or come back later, or come back never.

Tune into what your body tells you and *how* it tells you.

Your body is wise. You are the one you can trust.

Love,
    Anastasia

slip in a trick where there was trust,
sickness where it was sweet.
put pain inside of play,
and that's what this is.
that's what it is now – **here** – in me.

at first, i couldn't believe what
was happening —
how could he think ... ?
we're not ...?!
i'm a kid!
"the coolest kid" he ever met —
i swear, that's what he called me.

i tried to be cool.

they say to tell.
in those classes and at the doctor's,
they say it:
    "If a grown-up is hurting you or
    touching you in a way that feels
    bad or wrong, tell."
but my cousin isn't all the way grown-up
— he's only 22 — and i get hurt
all the time when i'm playing.

anyway,
what he did isn't what hurt most.
the hurt comes when i realize
i am afraid of him now.
like, **really** afraid
of the person i liked so much,
who i thought liked and loved me, too.

guess what?

being ~~ra~~ped by my not-quite-grown-up
cousin gave me powers.
i'm like one of the X-Men.
my spirit can fly while my body
stays down.
in my dreams i do it.
nightmares, too.
real life, too.
the name i gave myself is Ghost.
like all new superheroes,
i haven't learned to control my
powers yet.

but i'd rather be
a sorceress.

i have the best big sister you could want
in your whole life.
on their last birthday, they said,
    "From now on, call me Billie,
        and use these pronouns: they and them
        and he and him,"
which makes sense if you knew him
growing up.

i guess Billie needed our dad
to be all the way out of our lives
to be who he really is.
now that Dad is with his new family
in another state,
Billie can exist as his whole self.

Billie and our cousin were
the family daredevils.
they took turns swinging off
the willow branches into the deepest
part of the creek.

our cousin went away to be in the army
for a while, but
something happened and
he came back.

that's why he had
so much time
for me — hanging
out long days
by the creek
all summer,
like when we
were little and
Mom and Gramma
would take us.

Billie doesn't love our cousin anymore.
they wanna kill our cousin for
what he did to me.
Mom says don't kill him because
it will upset Gramma, and
Mom doesn't know yet how to tell her.
i say don't kill him because
that's my job.
well, not to kill him but to decide
what he deserves.

doesn't a person who made a mistake
deserve a chance to apologize
and be forgiven?
do they or don't they?
i believe my cousin does
and that we all do.

Billie's cheeks go dark as red wine
when i say stuff like that.
they disagree.

i wanna show you the good parts
of being with him
before this happened,
how fun it was.

picking and eating black raspberries
that grow along this path,
climbing around on the rocks
all up and down the creek,

balance beam-walking on the trees
that fell across the water.

he said i was the toughest kid
he ever met —
toughest and coolest.

i don't even know why
i started crying,
except that i never wanted
what ~~we were~~ doing
what **he** was doing!!

and it wasn't my idea.

that's when i got my powers.
i would be out here
when what was happening
was happening **there**.
new powers are unpredictable —
they flicker on and off.

my body was confused.
what body ??
who, me?
and then, BOOM.
i was **there**.
and i wanted
what was happening
to stop.

the last time it happened,
i cried,

and he laughed, just for a second.

and that's how i knew
he didn't care for me, which is
not the same as he hated me.
he doesn't!

once, my dad heard me say, "I don't care
for chocolate chip cookies."
this is true, by the way, even if
you can't believe it.
Dad liked that i didn't say
i hate chocolate chip cookies
because he says,
        "Hate is such a strong word."

but if you're doing something to someone
and they cry,
and that makes you laugh,
maybe you don't hate them —
but you don't care for them.
no matter what you believe about what
you are doing to them and
whether they should be crying about it,
you don't care for them if you laugh.
you don't care for them if you keep going
and say,
    "It's okay. Stay still."

it isn't okay.

my whole life,
my cousin never treated me like i was weak
before that.
he never acted like i couldn't do daring things
like Billie could always do,
or that i wouldn't want to.
then all of a sudden, my weakness
was everything.
like the air all around us was yelling.

STUPID! whyyy did
you TRUST him?!

why'd you wear that?
why'd you smile?
why did you LOVE him so much?

unless you wanted something to happen...
and i wanted to make the air
stop telling lies.
don't ruin it!
you're ruining it!

but it was too late when i realized
what he had ruined and how bad.

      i wonder what he thinks of me
now that i told my mother
what he did.
now that everything's ruined,
am i still cool?
am i still tough?
am i still a kid?

i wish i could tell more
about the things i can't tell anyone ever.
but i don't know the words
for the butterflies i get
when i'm scared or excited
that i get in the wrong place now.
a swirling good feeling is mixed up
with the smell of his shirts and being
too scared to move,
unable to breathe,
in the hot truck.
butterflies in the wrong place
make me feel sick ~~and something nice~~.
and i wanna throw up.
don't tell anyone that.
forget i said it.

when i told Mom what happened,
her face went →

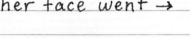

← and then

and then she cried.
and Billie and i cried, too.
like when Dad would say,
   "I'll give you something to cry about!"
well, guess what? this is **it**.
then Mom was quiet,
and she said she just needed to go
to the bathroom for a minute.

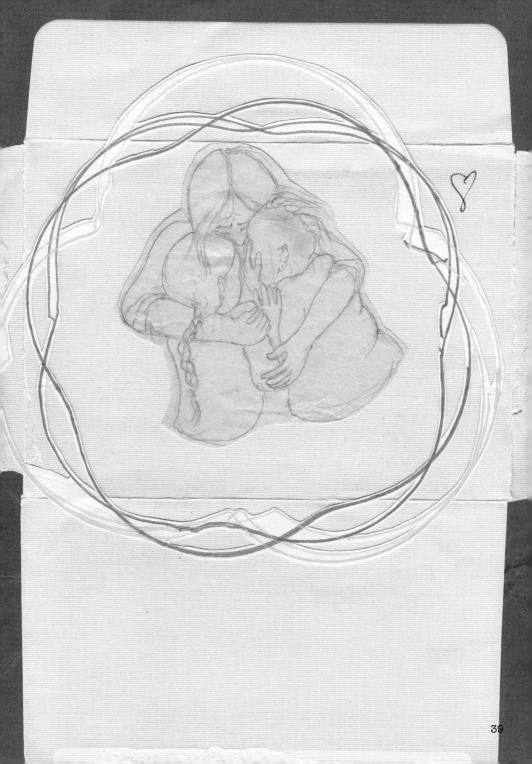

39

finally, she came back out.

"i'm happy you told me," she said.

but she did not look happy.

here comes the worse
part, but it wasn't
Mom's fault. next,
       she said,

"you can **never** go to the creek
with him again.
you can **never** go anywhere
with him again."

and i don't Know why but
that shocked me!
and i got SO mad
at her, my powers
Kicked in and —
whoosh — i was **gone!**

Mom got blurry.
my stomach felt like
i would throw up.

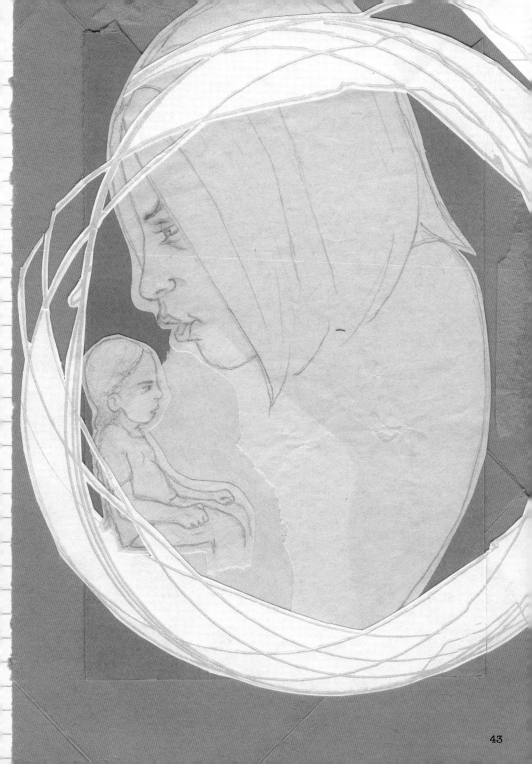

then i floated backward.
straight away from her!

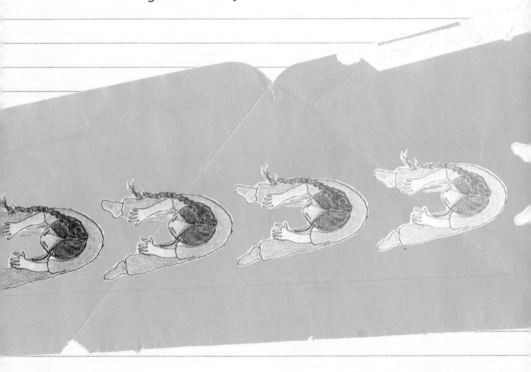

and because i don't Know how to control
my powers yet, i got stuck,

outside of myself.

for a while i watched them,
Billie and Mom.
they did life and i did floating.
they thought i was real-there
when i was only fake-there.

i was Ghost.

Mom took a class for a whole month
where they teach how to deal
with a real attacker.
She told us,
   "One teacher wears a huge, protective
   helmet and padded suit.
   The other teacher wears workout
   clothes and a whistle."

Mom learned how to strike **hard**, then
take a full breath and let it
all the way out, then
strike again **super hard**,
and breathe again.
she practices yelling
the loudest : NO!

this is something Mom has always
wanted to learn, she says.
because incest happened to her, too.
not exactly but enough the same so that
she said,
　　"This stops now in this family.
　　THIS STOPS NOW."

and the way she looked when she
said it and how loud
she said it kept me floating
outside my body
even longer.

but Billie loved learning the moves from Mom.
he practiced the NO and all of the strikes.
he even practiced the breathing in between.

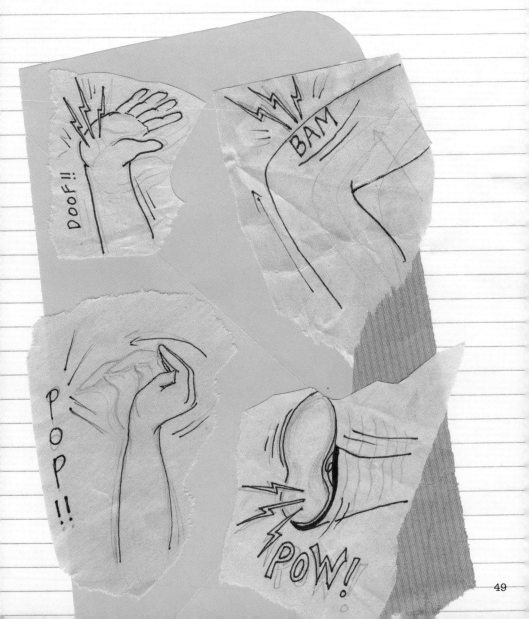

i hated those moves.
yes.
hated.

but here is where
hate comes in handy.
the feeling was so strong
it brought me back!

I didn't fight back!

I froze.
I never said "no."
I didn't want to get him in trouble
and I still don't.

You did not get him in trouble — *he* did!

Here's what I do know.
You're not the one to blame for what happened.
Also, fighting is only *one* choice.
Like it was your choice to come to me
    when you were ready.
That was brave.
You did what you could.
That's the most important thing.

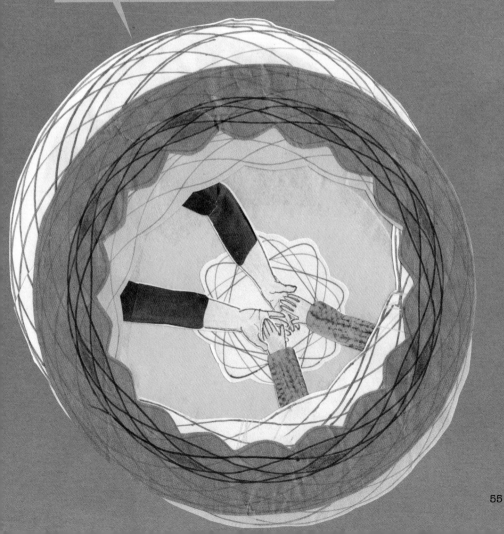

I want him to apologize for ruining the creek for me.

I don't think that can happen, Dawn. He won't admit he did it.

Can I take you to the creek?
I like black raspberries and climbing rocks.
We can reclaim it for you. We'll do a spell!

My girlfriend is
a witch.

Angeliska's a witch?!

Yes. A powerful one.

57

Are you gonna beat him up?!

Yes — if I get the chance!
And you can't stop me!
Somebody needs to make sure
he never does this again.

We'll make sure
he won't come near you
— or us — ever.

Don't get mad at what I say next.
Promise you won't be mad.

We promise.

Okay.

I know you hate him,
but I don't.

What he did was wrong but . . .
I just wish it could be like before.

I keep on missing him.

I'm gonna throw up.

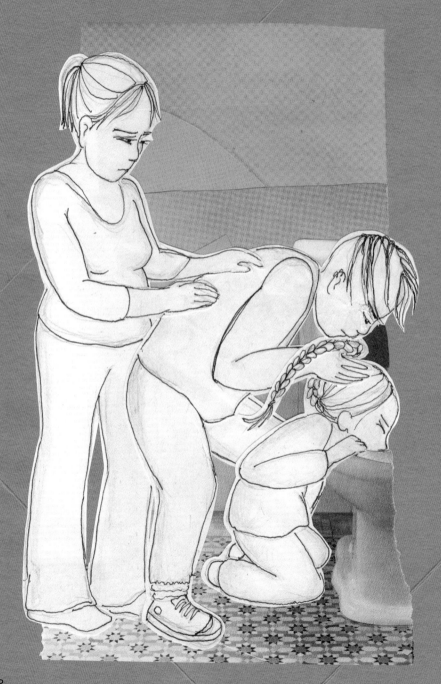

Let's sleep in my room tonight.

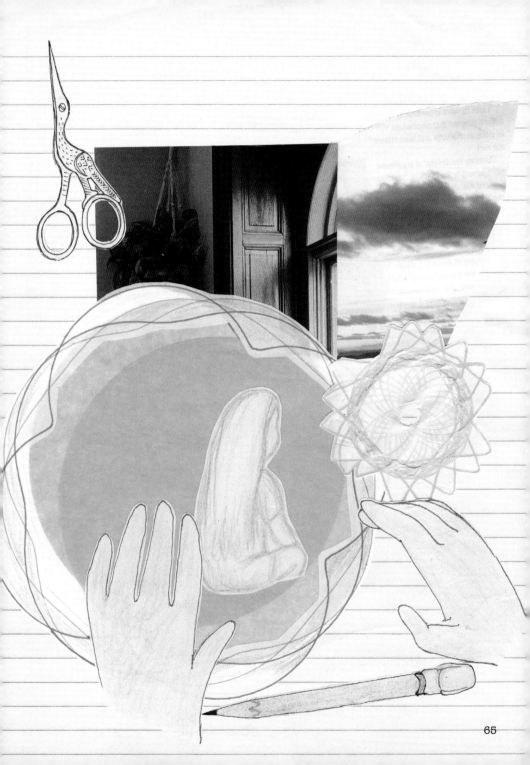

Angeliska cast a binding spell on
my cousin so he can do no more harm.

Billie adores
Angeliska.

And so do I.

By air and earth, by water and fire, so be you bound, as I desire. By three and nine, your power I bind, by moon and sun, my will be done.

Angeliska says my drawings
can be a practice in setting boundaries
and in discovering what
the boundaries even are.
what i want goes inside the circle.
what i don't want stays out.
what i want and don't want will change,
angeliska says, and i only need to
tune into myself to know the answers.
like listening to a song i love.
like listening for a voice from the earth,
speaking in vibrations.

Angeliska says to me,
     " YOU are the one you can trust. "

Mom told Gramma and my cousin's parents.
they say i'm overreacting
to something i misunderstood, or
i am making it up
to get attention.
they say all of the women
in this house
are crazy.

no one's telling Dad because he might
come back, and that would
be worse. Mom says he would either

   a. not believe us that it happened
              or
   b. blame her that it did
              or
   c. both.

          not helpful.

nobody wants to go to the police,
not even Billie.
why should i tell the story a thousand
times to people who need me
to prove he did it?

   besides, i don't want anyone from
   my family going to jail.

i'm learning my powers now.
when my feelings are more than
my body can hold, and also
when i'm scared or surprised,
i fly out.
when i put my hands on my belly
and remember that i have a body
and where it is,
i can return to it.
but it takes practice.
i still get surprised and get stuck
out there and get lost.
i can't stop flying out of myself,
so i practice returning.

i still fly on purpose in my dreams
though, for fun.

Angeliska flies beside me sometimes.

Mom and Billie understand why i get sad.
they let me heal and go through this.
we all Know i can do it.

i am the one
i can trust.

this is a story.

It's not my story exactly, and it's probably not yours. Our own stories can only be told by us—if we choose to tell them at all. (I often regret it.)

This book is not a how-to anything: cope, tell, parent, prevent, survive, or speak out against rape and abuse. It's a way for me to show some things I've wanted to show for a long time about what a sexual violation by a trusted someone can do to a kid.

Our ability to thrive and experience beauty, peace, and connection in spite of an experience like this only proves our radiance and resilience. It does not mean that what happened was "not that bad."

Don't believe it. Believe *you*. That's all.

offerings & ideas

When Dawn "floats" or "flies out" of herself, she's experiencing **dissociation, which is a physiological response to trauma, not a superpower.** Dawn relates to dissociation as a new ability and brings curiosity to how she might use it as an imaginative escape and form of astral projection. Nausea is also a common response to trauma. I share resources at the beginning and end of this book, including the names of those who have taught me about trauma and dissociation, about how to anchor yourself while still being an imaginative and fantastic person.

Both Dawn and her mother experience **not being believed when they disclose what has happened to them**. Billie, who is genderqueer, has no doubt confronted resistance and more aggressive reactions to his assertion of his true gender identity.

Think about a time when you were not believed. How would **being believed** have made a difference for you then?

revisit the images

throughout the story and notice all the ways
Dawn, Mom, Billie, and Angeliska **cope** with
what's happening. (Coping means managing
difficult feelings and experiences.)

Billie wants to avenge their sister using violence.
Billie is in pain. Notice how his pain shows up.

What are some ways **you** deal and cope with
stress, betrayal, or trauma in your life (whether
the trouble lands on you or someone close and
important to you)?

care vs. advice

Advice is telling people what to do, how to feel, and what they should've done or should do next. Unless asked for, advice is usually not that helpful. By contrast, words of care and support can be very healing. Here is an example of some healing words I'd offer Billie if I could: *I know you want more than anything to be able to keep your loved ones safe at all times. It was not your job to prevent this, and it is not your burden to avenge it.*

Are there any healing words and care—not advice—that you'd like to offer the characters in this story?

What are some healing words and care you might offer Dawn?

Mom?

Billie?

Angeliska?

how do you feel

about Dawn's grandmother and family of the cousin?

How about Dawn's father?

Imagine if you could write the next part of the story, where these characters make choices that you want them to make. How might these characters grow or change?

now

can you imagine any actions Dawn and Billie's cousin might take on his own behalf to stop causing harm and begin to address his own problems and pain?

If not, it's okay. You don't need to be the one to heal, fix, or redeem him—that's his job, not yours.

However, if you can imagine a path for him to do no more harm, be honest about what he did, make amends, and heal, you can name or draw the steps here.

we live in a culture

that **punishes**—*wow*, does it ever! People face harsh punishments at school, at home, in plenty of religions, and throughout society for breaking laws and rules—or even just standing out.

This same culture that punishes also excuses, ignores, and enables some people to face no consequences for law-breaking and harming behavior.

We watch this happen again and again. Too much depends on who occupies the seat of judgment, who interprets the rules and laws, and who holds the power to enforce them.

Justice is something else entirely.

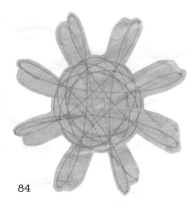

justice is: everybody gets what they need.

When it comes to reporting the crime to police, Dawn's wish is that none of her family members go to jail.

Can you imagine what Dawn's mother might do to both honor Dawn's wishes and move in ways that are just?

If you have ideas, you can explore them here.

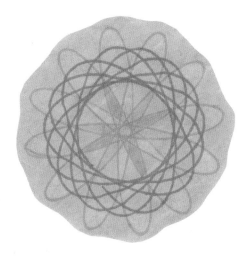

"**incest is practically unheard of** in families where parents share a mutual and equal position of authority, where feelings and opinions are aired openly in an atmosphere of trust, where children are respected, and where there are no secrets. Equality of power and position are key concepts in overcoming incest and other female* exploitation. Society must change its values, educational system and economic system. We can all help to play a role in this transformation."

—from *The Mother's Book: How to Survive the Incest of Your Child* by Carolyn M. Byerly

*We can treasure this insight and expand it here to
acknowledge that non-femme, cis boy, masculine-
passing, masculine-presenting, genderqueer,
nonbinary, gender-nonconforming, intersex,
and trans kids also experience sexual abuse and
exploitation. Non-femme and non-Mom parents
are also fully capable of creating an "atmosphere
of trust" and supporting their child through a
traumatic experience.

i took my first full-impact self-defense class

in 2000, at age twenty-nine. It changed me. Since that class, I completed every course offered through Prepare Inc. in New York City and trained to be an instructor. Over nearly two decades, as often as I could, I have worked to support students as they practice setting verbal boundaries while adrenalized and experience their body's ability to settle, speak, breathe, yell, and strike full power, then settle, breathe, and assess the most direct and available path to safety (whatever safety may be at any given time).

It is not possible to overstate the significance of this training in my ability to enjoy being exactly who and how I am. I am grateful to Prepare's co-owners for the joy that comes with knowing my own capacity for grace and fury, in balance and under pressure.

Donna and Karen,
I love you both fiercely.

love & gratitude to . . .

Tascha, you would have given everything to be able to save your sister — I thought of you so much as I made this book.

Alaina, you lavished me with care by funding a solitary space near my home where I could make this book and rest along the way.

Beloved readers, listeners, family, and friends:
Ava Budavari, Janah Boccio, Isabel Del Rosal,
Spencer Ellis, Jill Flowers, Amy Fusselman,
Lionel and Sabatino Higginbotham, Mirabelle Kirkland,
Jon Luongo, Maryann Luongo, Winter Miller,
Susan Mufson, Andrea Nemetz, yvette shipman,
Sharon Wyse, and my siblings, niblings, mom and dad.

Angeliska, you are the most
fantastic and true character in
this book, and your ways are magic.

When Jennifer asked Drew what he thought of my very first collages on grocery bag paper, he called them "exquisite" and gave us the confidence to launch the Ordinary Terrible Things series. Drew, I have benefited ever since from your loving artistry, which made each book beautiful and true to its purpose. Thank you for inviting Frances Ross to join us in fine-tuning the images. Frances, you add beauty in layers and depth.

editor & publisher

art director

These books are labor-intensive and expensive, and the stakes are always high — emotional, financial, cultural, and spiritual. Jennifer Baumgardner has braved every storm with me as a fierce and loyal friend, activist, and brilliant collaborator. Jennifer, I wish everyone could experience their work being valued the way you have valued me and mine.

Thank you for engaging the talented staff of Dottir — Erin, Kait, Kayla, Larissa, Noelle, Pearl, your children, and mine — whose steadiness and excellent instincts hone our messages and deepen our impact.

many of the spirograph

images throughout this story were made by my goddaughter Sara's daughters, **Eleanora**, nine, and **Leah**, eleven. All spirograph designs were made using the Spirograph Die-Cast Collectors Set, 2015 Hasbro Edition.

I chose the spirograph design because it let me create borders that are beautiful, colorful, and imperfect. The only way to get that loopy, gorgeous pattern is by holding the pen lightly-but-firmly and focusing all the way around on the spot where the jagged edges fit neatly together. **It is not possible to behold the beauty of the boundary while I'm making it**; the ring that keeps the border must stay still. Places where the pen jumped or the pieces slid out often become my favorite part. Something happened there—or didn't. Look, you can see it: the stop and restart, the tremor before it gets smooth again. I don't get better and better at it. I still mess them up. Has there ever been a better metaphor for learning boundaries than this? Not to me.

here is a place

where you can practice your boundaries. What you want from anyone who wants to be in relationship with you goes inside the circle. Everything else stays out. Some examples: *"Care about me. Listen to my words. Read my body language. Be curious about me."*

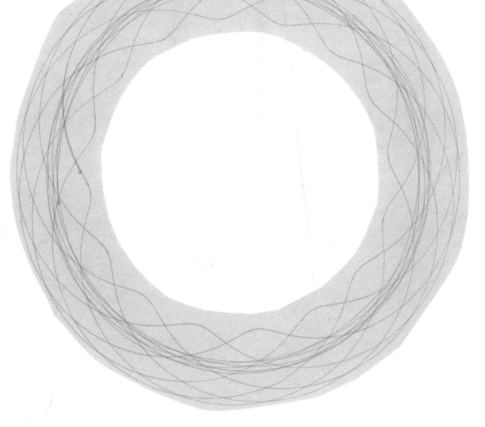

i made this story by drawing

on the brilliance and lessons I learn from other artists, writers, healers, and experts in their field. I offer their names with gratitude and to credit each one for helping me do what I needed to do. If you want to learn more, seek them out.

Lynda Barry
(what is an image? and ways to stay)

Judith Herman
(incest, trauma, memory, dissociation)

Resmaa Menakem
(somatic practice, the Five Anchors)

Clarissa Pinkola Estés
(healing the deep psyche, She Who Knows)

Prepare Inc.
(breathe, settle, "ready position")

Love WITH Accountability:
Digging Up the Roots of Child Sexual Abuse,
an anthology edited by Aishah Shahidah Simmons
(centers Black survivors, radical healing,
and accountability)

adrienne maree brown, Shira Hassan
and Prentis Hemphill
(boundaries, embodiment, transformative justice)

Rev. angel Kyodo williams
(own-belonging, return to self)

In loving memory of

Tierne